W9-DES-314

WOMEN in the U.S. ARMED FORCES

Women of the U.S. Air Force
AIMING HIGH

by Heather E. Schwartz

Consultant:
Raymond L. Puffer, PhD
Historian, Retired
Edwards Air Force Base History Office

CAPSTONE PRESS
a capstone imprint

Snap Books are published by Capstone Press,
151 Good Counsel Drive, P.O. Box 669, Mankato, Minnesota 56002.
www.capstonepub.com

 Books published by Capstone Press are manufactured with paper
containing at least 10 percent post-consumer waste.

Library of Congress Cataloging-in-Publication Data
Schwartz, Heather E.
  Women of the U.S. Air Force : Aiming High / by Heather E. Schwartz.
    p. cm. — (Snap. Women in the U.S. armed forces)
  Includes bibliographical references and index.
  Summary: "Describes the past, present, and future of women in the U.S. armed forces"—Provided by publisher.
  ISBN 978-1-4296-5449-4 (library binding)
  1. United States. Air Force—Women—Juvenile literature. I. Title. II. Series.

UG834.W65S44 2011
358.40082'0973—dc22   2010040749

Editor: Mari Bolte
Designers: Juliette Peters and Kyle Grenz
Production Specialist: Laura Manthe

Photo Credits:
Corbis: Bettmann, 16, 17; Getty Images Inc.: Time Life Pictures/Peter Stackpole, 12; NASA,
20; Photo courtesy Air Force Flight Test Center History Office, 10; Photo courtesy of Woman's
Collection, Texas Woman's University, 11; U.S. Air Force photo, 13, 15, 21; U.S. Air Force photo by
A1C Greg L. Davis, 23; Airman 1st Class Stephenie Wade, 26; Master Sgt. Demetrius Lester, 22;
Master Sgt. Maurice Hassel, 7; Senior Airman Nathanael Callon, 25; SSGT Thompson, 6; Staff Sgt.
Desiree N. Palacios, 19; Staff Sgt. Michael Holzworth, 8; Staff Sgt. Richard Williams, 27; Staff Sgt.
Tony R. Tolley, 5; Tech. Sgt. Lindsey Maurice, cover; U.S. Marine Corps photo by Lance Cpl. Karl
Launius, 9

Artistic Effects:
Shutterstock: Maugli

Printed in the United States of America in North Mankato, Minnesota.
092010   005933CGS11

TABLE of CONTENTS

CHAPTER 1

FAST FLIGHT

In 2006 the U.S. Air Force **aerial** demonstration **squadron** known as the Thunderbirds announced its newest pilots. Major Nicole Malachowski didn't expect to be on the list. She was a fighter pilot and had the skills, but Thunderbirds were always men. She was shocked when she found out she had been chosen. She also felt honored. She would be the first female Thunderbird pilot in history.

Before her first performance, Nicole practiced. It was important that Nicole be comfortable in the plane. She flew an F-16 jet, the type of plane used by the Thunderbirds. The F-16 can reach speeds of 1,500 miles (2,414 kilometers) an hour.

She also needed to prove herself to the other pilots. The group practiced moves such as 360-degree rolls and flying upside down.

During the show season, Nicole traveled eight months out of the year to represent the U.S. Air Force across the country. While on tour, she and her fellow pilots gave speeches. They talked about their service at schools. As a girl, Nicole had grown up with a seemingly impossible dream. Now she was a role model for young girls around the country.

aerial: a trick that is done in the air

squadron: an official military unit

Pilots like Nicole Malachowski fly with the Thunderbirds for two and a half years.

"The message to all young Americans is that it's great to have a dream. It's great to have goals," she has said. "I hope that when they see the Air Force Thunderbirds, they realize they can achieve any dream, and that a great team to have is certainly the Air Force."

Childhood Dreams

Nicole was just 5 years old when she watched her first air show. She saw the F-4 Phantom planes shoot over her head and knew that she wanted to fly too. From that point on, she wanted to be a fighter pilot. She decorated her room with fighter planes. It was 1979, and women weren't allowed to be fighter pilots. But young Nicole didn't know that. Even after her sixth grade teacher informed her of the law, Nicole wouldn't be stopped. She began working toward her goal with the support of her family.

Nicole was 12 when she joined the Civil Air Patrol. Through the program, Nicole won a scholarship that paid for her flying lessons. She studied at the North Las Vegas Airport near her home. She took lessons and flew her first solo mission while in high school.

The power and grace of the F-4 Phantom jets led Nicole to follow her dream.

Nicole (right) meets fans after a Thunderbird demonstration

Nicole also participated in the Reserve Officer Training Corps (ROTC) program. She became the highest-ranked **cadet** in the country.

After high school, Nicole went on to the U.S. Air Force Academy. Even if she couldn't fight in the air, she knew she wanted to work with planes. While she was there, the law changed. The Air Force began training female fighter pilots.

cadet: a young person who is training to become a member of the armed forces

The Thunderbirds have toured the United States since 1953.

Nicole graduated fourth in her class from the Air Force Academy. She soon realized her dream of becoming a fighter pilot. She served as an instructor and a flight commander. She also flew **combat** missions in Iraq and Kosovo.

Joining the Thunderbirds was not something Nicole had considered doing earlier in her career. But she had 1,300 hours of flight time. Her polished record as a pilot meant Nicole could apply. She sent a letter explaining her desire to become a Thunderbird. She also described her flight history and her service in the Air Force. In addition, she added five letters of recommendation. Next, she showed off her talents as a pilot. Finally she was interviewed by the Thunderbirds.

combat: fighting between people or armies

Nicole proved she was the best person for the job. Her first Thunderbird show was in 2006 at Fort Smith, Arkansas. It was a historic moment, though most people probably didn't realize it. Audience members were surprised to learn a woman had been flying one of the jets. She participated in about 140 Thunderbird performances. Nicole was happy she could be there to inspire people simply by doing her job.

The men and women of the Air Force must work together as a team to complete their missions. "There is no way that any one person can do this job alone," Nicole has said about her role as an Air Force pilot. "It is an absolute team effort."

Nicole spent more than 200 days on the road with the Thunderbirds.

Maj Nicole Malachowski
Right Wing

CHAPTER 2

HISTORY IN MOTION

Women have been flying military planes since even before the United States Air Force existed. The Women's Airforce Service Pilots (WASP) allowed women to fly during World War II (1939–1945). It was formed in 1943 thanks to Jacqueline Cochran and Nancy Harkness Love.

Jacqueline Cochran

Nancy Harkness Love

Jacqueline was famous for winning air races and setting many flight records. Throughout her career, she was often labeled as the world's most outstanding female flyer. Nancy was not as well known, but she was a skilled pilot. She performed tasks such as testing landing gear and marking water towers.

Both women believed the United States would do better in the war if women were allowed to serve as pilots. Working separately, they contacted President Franklin D. Roosevelt, first lady Eleanor Roosevelt, and several high-ranking military officials. Eventually they combined their efforts to form the WASP.

Female flyers learn to read symbols and weather maps, 1943

The WASP flew 78 kinds of aircraft for the Army Air Corps.

WASP women filled roles that included test pilots, towing targets, aerial demonstrators, and flight instructors. Thirty-eight WASP women died while serving during World War II. But despite their service, WASP was not a recognized branch of the military. The WASP had to pay for their own food, lodging, and uniforms. After serving, they did not receive retirement benefits. Those who died were not given a military burial.

By December 1944, the WASP program was shut down. Female military pilots were officially grounded.

Earning Rights

In 1947 President Harry S. Truman signed the National Security Act into law. The law improved the country's military defense. It created a National Security Council and a Central Intelligence Agency (CIA). It also made the U.S. Air Force a separate military branch, equal to the Army and Navy.

The following year, Truman signed the Women's Armed Services **Integration** Act. Female **veterans** could receive military burials and other benefits. But they could not serve in combat.

On July 8, 1948, Esther M. Blake became the first woman to join the U.S. Air Force. Esther and her fellow female **recruits** became part of the Women in the Air Force (WAF) program. They trained separately from men. Although they were seen as equals, they were still expected to be feminine. Members of the WAF had to take classes on manners, makeup, hair care, posture, and movement. Many went on to serve in office jobs and in the Air Force Nurse Corps.

integrate: the practice of including people of all races or genders

veteran: someone who has served in the armed forces

recruit: new members to a group

In its early days, WAF was limited to 4,000 regular members and 300 officers.

3743RD
WAF
TRAINING
SQUADRON

Over the years, more Air Force positions opened up to women. By 1973 women were working in communications, electronics, and engineering. They continued to take jobs previously held only by men. But they were still not allowed to train or serve as pilots.

One of the first Air Force Academy classes to allow women, 1976

Gaining Respect

In the late 1970s, WAF squadrons were phased out. Women in the Air Force no longer had to belong to a separate program. They could join the regular Air Force. They also received the same training as men.

In 1976 the Air Force Academy allowed women to attend for the first time. And the Air Force began training women as pilots again. Women who joined the Air Force did not have an easy time. But men at the academy were willing to see if women could meet the academy's high standards.

The co-ed classes had a hard time bonding. Some men thought the women got special treatment. Hard feelings grew, and 44 percent of the men in the first co-ed class dropped out before their graduation.

It would take time to create a system that was fair to both men and women. Still, women were gaining opportunities and credit for their efforts. In 1977 WASP was finally recognized as part of the military. President Jimmy Carter signed a law that gave former WASP members official status and rights as veterans. Three years later, 97 women graduated from the Air Force Academy. By 1989 nearly every job open to men in the Air Force was also open to women.

The first 10 women to enter military flight training, 1977

CHAPTER 3

AIMING HIGH

Training For Flight

More than 39,000 recruits pass through Lackland Air Force Base in San Antonio, Texas, every year. Nearly 20 percent of those recruits are women. Lackland is the Air Force's only **basic training** facility.

Basic training lasts eight and a half weeks. Until 2008 basic training was two weeks shorter. Today additional war skills are taught during these added 14 days.

Recruits conduct drills with their squads. They practice using, cleaning, and assembling weapons. They learn first aid. Everything they learn will prepare them for combat. During the fourth week of training, the recruits practice these skills in a mock **deployment**. They learn to work as a team against enemy attacks.

To graduate, all recruits must meet physical fitness standards. Women must run 1.5 miles (2.4 kilometers) in less than 16 minutes, 22 seconds. They are also expected to do 18 push-ups in one minute and 38 sit-ups in one minute. After graduation they've earned the right to wear their blue uniforms and be called Airmen.

The term "Airman" applies to both men and women.

basic training: the first training period for people who join the military

deploy: to position troops for combat

Female Airmen use their knowledge to achieve more than ever before. They have mastered the skies. Now they want to master the stars. About 80 current and former astronauts have worn Air Force uniforms, and 49 of these were women. Brigadier General Susan Helms and Colonel Eileen Collins were among them. Susan was serving in the Air Force when NASA chose her to train as an astronaut. In 1993 she became the first U.S. military woman in space.

Eileen was working as a special test pilot when she was selected. She joined NASA about the same time as Susan. In 1999 she became the first woman to run a space shuttle. Because of these women, other female Airmen have the chance to go into space.

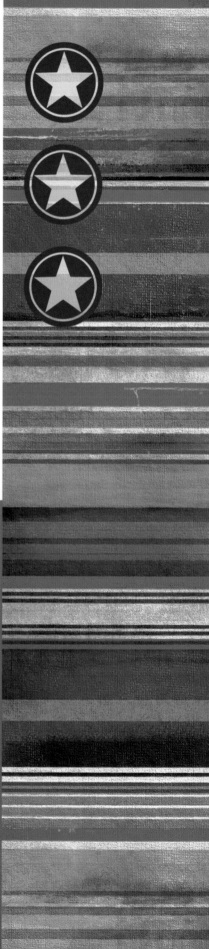

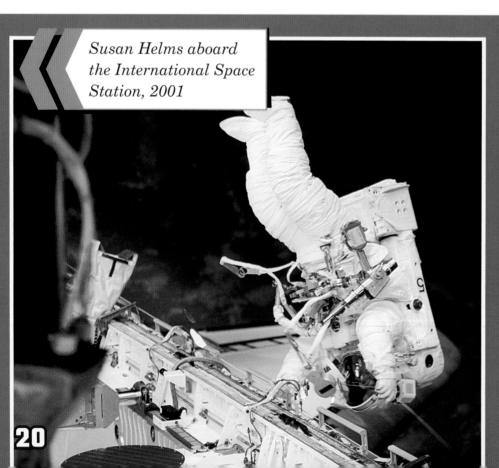

Susan Helms aboard the International Space Station, 2001

Women were banned from flying in air combat until 1991. Martha McSally began her combat flight training in 1993.

Women in Combat

Many Air Force pilots have flown fighter jets, gunships, and bombers in war zones. Lieutenant Colonel Martha McSally was among the first female fighter pilots. She flew an A-10 Thunderbolt II, or Warthog, in Kuwait. In 2004 Martha became the first female commander of a fighter squadron. Today there are more than 14,000 pilots in the Air Force. About 3,700 fly fighter jets. And 70 of the fighter pilots are women.

Female Airmen also connect with the communities they serve. Senior Airman Vanessa Velez saw that firsthand in Afghanistan. She got to know local children while driving military vehicles through enemy territory. The children took an interest in the female soldier. Their bond allowed both Afghans and military personnel a chance to see each other as people and not enemies. Many had questions for Velez and talked to her about their concerns for their families.

Vanessa Velez drove in at least 120 convoys during the year she served in Afghanistan.

Exceptional Service

Female Airmen have served overseas in both Operation Enduring Freedom (2001–present) and Operation Iraqi Freedom (2003–2010). They performed duties in dangerous territory on a regular basis. Sometimes they were attacked. They risked their lives to defend their country and finish their missions.

Airmen must be ready for deployment at all times.

Women in war zones also help others during emergencies. In 2010, 83 Afghani villagers were caught in a flash flood. They huddled together on a sandbar in the middle of a river. The normally calm, shallow water was 20 feet (6.1 meters) deep in some spots. The water was flowing fast and threatened to destroy the village.

Helicopters were flown in to save the villagers. The pilots faced many challenges. First, they had only a rough idea of where the village was. Second, they were flying during a dust storm, and it was hard to see. Finally, the villagers had to be searched before boarding. Male Airmen could not search the female villagers. But Technical Sergeant Erica Thompson was on hand to do the job.

CHAPTER 4

FLYING into the FUTURE

Facing Challenges

Women in the Air Force continue to face challenges. There are still some jobs done by few or no women. Women make up 20 percent of the Air Force. But only 8 percent of them pursue technical careers, such as engineering. Even qualified women are less likely to follow a technical career. One reason is that there are few female role models for young women. And mechanics and engineering are seen as male jobs.

But that is slowly changing. Opportunities for women exist in fields, like engineering, communications, and electronics. Female Airmen currently serving in these fields are proving that women can succeed in technical jobs too.

Female Airmen serving in the Middle East are role models to young girls in Afghanistan and Iraq.

The Ground Combat Debate

Female Airmen are allowed to fight in the air. But women in all military branches are not allowed to fight in ground combat. However, women serving in the Middle East cannot avoid serving in combat zones. Women work in combat zones and are acknowledged by their superior officers. Women driving trucks, providing security, or working in the area are targeted by enemies.

An Airman practices loading weapons onto a jet

Building on the Legacy

Women have served the Air Force since its creation. They showed early on that women could do the same office jobs as men. Thirty years ago, women wanted to be full-time flyers. Twenty years ago, they dreamed of becoming fighter pilots. Today women in the Air Force are doing that and much more.

Staff Sergeant Esther Blake joined an hour after the Air Force was formed in 1948. Major General Jeanne Holm became the first female Air Force General in 1973. The first woman aerial gunner was Airman 1st Class Vanessa Dobos in 2003. And in 2006, Nicole Malachowski soared the skies as the first female Thunderbird pilot.

Female Airmen take on challenges and give their best service to the Air Force. Their history of hard work and dedication makes it possible for today's women to do the same. Women can join the Air Force, go after their career of choice, and give their all in military service.

Female Airmen serve their country in the skies and on the ground around the world.

FAST FACTS

⭐ The 27th Fighter Squadron is the Air Force's oldest squadron. It was formed June 15, 1917.

⭐ WASPs flew 60 million miles (97 million kilometers) during their service in World War II.

⭐ More than 25,000 women applied to become WASPs. Only 1,830 were accepted to train.

TIMELINE

1943 **1947** **1948** **1976**

The Women's Armed Services Integration Act is signed into law.

The U.S. Air Force is established under the National Security Act.

The Air Force begins training women as pilots again.

The Women's Airforce Service Pilots (WASP) is formed.

⭐ The Air Force integrated basic training in 1949. This encouraged more African-Americans to enlist.

⭐ In 1978 Major General Jeanne Holm became the first female Air Force general. She was also the first female major general in any of the armed forces.

⭐ In 2008 about 70 out of 3,700 fighter pilots in the U.S. Air Force were women.

WASP is recognized by law as part of the U.S. military.

Female Airmen are deployed to serve in Iraq.

1977   **2001**   **2003**   **2010**

Female Airmen are deployed to serve in Afghanistan.

Veteran WASP receive the Congressional Gold Medal.

GLOSSARY

aerial (AYR-ee-uhl)—a trick that is done in the air

basic training (BAY-sik TRANE-ing) the first training period for people who join the military; basic training is sometimes called boot camp.

cadet (kuh-DET)—a young person who is training to become a member of the armed forces

combat (KOM-bat)—fighting between people or armies

deploy (deh-PLOY)—to position troops for combat

integrate (in-tuh-GRAY-te)—the practice of including people of all races or genders in schools and other public places

recruit (ri-KROOT)—new members to a group

squadron (SKWAHD-ruhn)—an official military unit

veteran (VET-ur-uhn)—someone who has served in the armed forces

READ MORE

Braulick, Carrie A. *The U.S. Air Force Thunderbirds*. The U.S. Armed Forces. Mankato, Minn.: Capstone Press, 2006.

David, Jack. *Air Force Air Commandos*. Torque: Armed Forces. Minneapolis, Minn.: Bellwether Media, 2009.

Loveless, Antony. *Air War*. Crabtree Contact. New York: Crabtree Publishing Company, 2008.

INTERNET SITES

FactHound offers a safe, fun way to find Internet sites related to this book. All of the sites on FactHound have been researched by our staff.

Here's all you do:

Visit *www.facthound.com*

Type in this code: 9781429654494

Check out projects, games and lots more at
www.capstonekids.com

INDEX

ABOUT the AUTHOR

Heather E. Schwartz is the author
of several books for Capstone Press.
She lives in upstate New York with
her husband and young son.